CW00666705

Short Stories

M Gullash

Martin Gallagher

Short Stories

Olympia Publishers
London

www.olympiapublishers.com
OLYMPIA PAPERBACK EDITION

Copyright © Martin Gallagher 2020

The right of Martin Gallagher to be identified as author of
this work has been asserted in accordance with sections 77 and 78
of the Copyright, Designs and Patents Act 1988.

All Rights Reserved

No reproduction, copy or transmission of this publication
may be made without written permission.
No paragraph of this publication may be reproduced,
copied or transmitted save with the written permission of the
publisher, or in accordance with the provisions
of the Copyright Act 1956 (as amended).

Any person who commits any unauthorised act in relation to
this publication may be liable to criminal
prosecution and civil claims for damage.

A CIP catalogue record for this title is
available from the British Library.

ISBN: 978-1-78830-824-3

This is a work of fiction.
Names, characters, places and incidents originate from the writer's
imagination. Any resemblance to actual persons, living or dead, is
purely coincidental.

First Published in 2020

Olympia Publishers
Tallis House
2 Tallis Street
London
EC4Y 0AB

Printed in Great Britain

Dedication

I would like to dedicate the book to my son, Patrick

Two Hearts Entwined: Remember Me

Chapter One

Prince Michael of Carponol lay in bed, his whole body soaked in sweat. He tossed and turned in a fever-filled delirium. He had remained in a semi-comatose state ever since being thrown from his horse two weeks prior to the announcement of his engagement to Princess Amelia for Valantia. The Queen's personal physicians said his injuries healed successfully. They couldn't understand why he hadn't made a full recovery by now. Queen Phoebe sat at her son's bedside, her face drawn and tear-stained, his yet-to-be-fiancée sat by the bedside also. Head bowed, her eyes covered with a pretty lace kerchief. Princess Amelia's eyes were not red-rimmed, however, nor were her cheeks wet with tears of sorrow. Instead, her expression hid one of frustration and anger. She waited and schemed for so long to become prince Michael's wife, a step nearer her ultimate goal of becoming the queen of all Carponol and Valantia. Now it seemed, with the prince on the cusp of death, her ambition would be denied to her. Queen Phoebe sent word to all the physicians throughout Carponol and Valantia all who came couldn't explain why the prince had not recovered; his condition only worsened by the day. The queen stood, reaching a decision; she left the prince's bedchamber to find the general of her army.

"Send men out to find the old mystic Nathanial," the queen told the general. Queen Phoebe didn't believe in the mystics and their magic, but this was her last resort. She was desperate enough to try anything to cure her son of his malady. The following day, the mystic arrived the queen led him into prince's bedchamber.

"Please, help my son. I beg you; I will reward you with anything you want, only please help him," Queen Phoebe pleaded.

Nathanial nodded, stroking his white beard as he looked over the prone prince with a careful eye. He touched his fevered brow and held his limp hand, finally checking the healed wound in the prince's side. The mystic frowned for several minutes; he stood over the bed observing the prince who moaned and tossed fitfully in his delirium. "I cannot help the prince," the mystic said finally.

The queen became distraught, "Please, there must be something you can I beg you." The queen held the mystic's hand, tears blinding her vision.

Nathanial raised a hand, sympathy showing in his wrinkled, aged face. "I know someone who may be able to help."

A glimmer of hope shone in the queen's eyes, "Who? Who can help? I'll send men to bring this person here at once."

The mystic's eyes narrowed, "In the vale forest that separates Carponol from Valantia lives the enchantress Melina. Find her. If you can persuade her, she may be able to help cure the prince. But be aware, she may exact a heavy price for her assistance."

The queen sent all the men she could spare to search the forest for the enchantress. While the scheming princess sent her own men hoping to find the enchantress first. The soldiers searched for many days in vain. Finally, one day, the enchantress came to the castle herself wearing a grey cloak and hood under which she was dressed all in white. The hood covered her head and hid most of her face from view. Long straw-coloured hair hung loosely around her shoulders. Many believed the enchantress to be a wizened old crone. Others said she was hideously disfigured, and that's why she always hid her face. Anyone who met her only got a fleeting glimpse of her face. None truly knew what the enchantress looked like. Melina walked up to the castle gates with a natural grace and confidant air. "I am Melina; I believe the Queen has been looking for me," she announced.

At that moment, the queen sat at her son's bedside; a soldier rushed to inform the queen that the enchantress stood at the castle gates awaiting entrance. Queen Phoebe rose to her feet, commanding that Melina be allowed in immediately, and rushed to greet her as did the princess as soon as she heard the news.

"Enchantress, welcome to my home; you are my last hope," the queen humbly beseeched.

The princess finally arriving a little later stood beside the queen breathless; giving the enchantress a frosty look as she tried to peer under the hood covering most of Melina's face. "I hope you will be able to cure my poor husband," the princess said.

The enchantress stared questioningly at the princess, "Husband? I am not aware the prince is already married."

The princess huffed her tone indifferent, "Oh, it is only a formality isn't it, Your Majesty," the princess began turning to the queen who nodded absently in agreement. She turned back to face the enchantress again as she continued in a condescending tone. "Once you hopefully cure him, we will be married eventually. You can cure him, can't you?"

"The answer to both your questions is, nothing is for certain," Melina said enigmatically.

The princess batted her eyelashes and frowned, puzzled by Melina's answer. "I thought I only asked if you can cure him."

Melina nodded, "You did." She turned to face the queen, ignoring any further comment from the now vexed princess, "Now if you please Your Majesty take me to the prince so that I can see what is required of me."

The queen led the way to the prince's bedchamber with the princess following close behind. Melina entered the bedchamber looking around the room before letting her eyes rest on the prince. She turned to face the queen and princess stood by the door. "I need to be alone with him, Your Majesty; none may enter until I leave," Melina said.

The queen looked troubled, "Well, I'm not sure... can you really cure what ails him?"

"How do we know you won't bewitch him or do something to make him worse," the princess put in petulantly as the queen hesitated.

Melina ignored the princess and addressed the queen, "Queen Phoebe, I can cure the prince, but if you can't trust me alone with him then I'll be on my way," Melina bowed.

"No, wait, all right; are you sure you can cure him?"

Melina nodded, "I'm certain, but there will be consequences."

The queen frowned, "Consequences?"

Melina shrugged her shoulders, "As I said, Majesty, you would have to trust me. I cannot say yet what the consequences may be; I will know better when I'm done."

The queen pursed her lips, considering as Melina waited patiently. "Very well, we will wait outside, but I'll post guards on the door just in case."

Melina gave a deep bow, "Thank you for trusting me. Your Majesty, now if you please leave me alone with him so that I can do my work." Melina knew the queen didn't really trust her, but was left with no choice if she wanted her son cured.

The queen nodded; she took the princess's arm, and they both left before Amelia could say anything more to upset the enchantress. Queen Phoebe did not look happy with leaving Melina alone with her son. She surmised the enchantress wanted to keep the secret of her art; thus, the need to be alone with the prince. She hoped that was the case and that there was no other disreputable motive; she couldn't help but worry for her son. There was much at stake for herself and the prince; he was, after all, the future heir to the throne.

Chapter Two

Alone in the room, Melina once more looked around; she could learn something about the prince by how he kept his room. The bedchamber was spacious, neat and tidy. A fire burned in the hearth at the far side of the room – the bed situated on the opposite side. To the right there was an arched window. Melina went to the window, unlatching and opening it. A draft of cold air entered. It was near mid-winter and snow lay in the courtyard below and fell from a grey sky. Melina went to the now dying fire – only embers remained; she past her hand over the fire, and it flared into life again. Finally, she took off her cloak and hood as she approached the prince. Melina opened a small bag tied to her waist and retrieved a dagger with strange twisted markings engraved on the hilt. She held the dagger in both hands above the prince passing it over the length of the prince's body; then, undoing her bodice, she made a shallow cut on her breast above her heart. She repeated the same for the prince, letting the blood from both their cuts mix together. Wiping the dagger clean, she replaced it in her bag and fastened her bodice.

Melina placed a hand on prince's fevered brow; a glow emitted between her fingers. She kept her hand on the prince's brow for several minutes. She could not help but look at the prince, studying his features, though his face was a little thinner and paler than she would expect him to look when at full health. He still looked handsome with slick black hair, blue eyes, a well-formed nose and his chin covered in several weeks stubble. She moved her hand to his side. As she did, his eyes fluttered open, and he gazed up into the face he thought to be an angel. A face white as snow, yet with the slightest touch of red in the cheeks with eyes as green as emeralds and long blonde hair.

"Who..." he rasped before falling unconscious again.

"Hush now, sleep. All will be well soon... Remember me," the enchantress whispered. She noted the wound on the prince's breast had gone. Melina sat by his bed, exhausted, she waited and slept. She woke to a knock on the door glancing at the prince, barely making out his features in the fading light. Seeing his colour return and fever gone, she rose to don her cloak and hood once more and went to open the door.

The queen waited anxiously, wringing her hands – there was no sign of the princess – the hour being late, she had retired to her bed. "How is he? Did your magic work?"

The enchantress nodded, "Yes, he will be well enough to be up and about soon. It was harder than I expected, though."

"What do you mean? Is it about the consequences?"

The enchantress nodded gravely, "It did not work fully; however, he will regain his health quickly though it won't last."

The queen frowned her face creased in worry lines, "I don't understand what you're trying to tell me?"

"He will stay well for a time then the malady will return."

"For how long... I thought you said you could cure him? All you're offering him is a stay of execution." The queen said in an accusing tone, her anger rising.

"He has a year before it returns, unless..."

The queen took a breath to control herself as she glared at Melina, "What! Unless what," she demanded.

"He must find his true love by the year's end, or he will begin to fall ill once more, and this time he will die," the enchantress said solemnly.

The queen stood dumbfounded for a moment then raised arms in exasperation, "Well, that isn't a problem; he is to marry the princess – she is his true love."

"If that is so then you have nothing to worry about, Your Majesty. I bid you farewell," with that, the enchantress left. Once outside the castle, she stood looking back for a moment. A chill wind blew. Melina wrapped her cloak tight around herself. Snow still fell from a darkened sky. Melina retrieved a small crystal orb from her bag, passing her free hand over the orb while chanting – The enchantress vanished.

Prince Michael sat up in bed colour returning to his cheeks though face still gaunt. "I feel much better now; stop fussing so much, Mother."

The queen sat at his bedside – the strain of the last weeks not entirely gone though – she breathed a little easier. "I hope you ate all the food I had sent to you," she paused a faint smile crossing her face. "You need to build your strength up again, doesn't he? Your Highness... He is so pale and thin."

Princess Amelia smiled demurely, "My poor prince has indeed lost weight, Your Majesty. We must be sure to feed him well from now on."

The prince frowned a faraway look in his eyes and appeared not to notice what the princess said, "I keep seeing a woman," he paused as if trying to remember something. "I'm not sure if it was just a fever-filled dream, but she looked familiar, and she had the face of an angel... it.. it... seemed so real."

The queen and the princess looked at each other knowingly, "It was probably me you saw; after all, I attended you every day as did your mother. Isn't that right, Your Majesty?" the princess put in hastily.

The queen nodded several times,"Yes, Yes, that must be it. The princess has been very supportive and a great help to both of us during your illness."

The prince seemed unsure; he frowned, "Well, thank you, Mother and you also Amelia, for standing by me. By the way, how did I become so gravely ill from a mere fall and how I did so suddenly get cured? From what you tell me, I was at death's door."

The queen looked flustered, "Oh, well... erm, I'm not really sure about the fall; I guess it was just a complication resulting from it as to your cure. Well, I had the best physicians in our countries attend you; they were bound to find a cure eventually."

The prince nodded thinking, yet something still nagged at him. However, feeling a little tired, he let the matter drop, "Oh, well I suppose that's it."

The queen and princess left the prince to rest a while. While the queen went to attend to the day's court affairs, Princess Amelia headed for her chambers; her mind racing, she paid little attention to those around her. Entering her chambers, she confronted a mysterious man in black. "I'm surprised you have the nerve to show your face here again after the last debacle," the princess snapped angrily.

Princess Amelia pouted at him, nostrils flaring, "So how do propose redeeming yourself?"

The man smiled unpleasantly; he held out a vial containing a blueish coloured liquid for the princess, "Here, Your Highness, this time I promise it will work."

The princess snatched the vial, giving the man a meaningful look, "It better work this time for your sake."

He bowed still smiling and left the princess alone to her thoughts; stealthily keeping to the shadows, he made his way out of the castle unseen.

Chapter Three

The spring ball saw the announcement of betrothal between Prince Mickael of Carponol and Princess Amelia of Valantia. The peoples of both countries rejoiced and celebrated the forthcoming wedding which was to be held later in the year. The couple seemed happy and content, yet something still troubled the prince. He had given up asking about the time he was ill and about the woman in his dream. Every time he tried to bring it up, both his mother and Amelia changed the subject. He felt sure now it wasn't Amelia. The woman in his dream was far more beautiful than Amelia in his eyes, and she seemed warmer, more caring and compassionate than anyone he ever met before. He wondered if he was deluding himself making up some fantastic romantic fantasy in his mind. At the same time, he wondered why he would need to make up such a grand fantasy. He loved Amelia, and that should be enough for him; he needed to rid himself of such fanciful nonsense and concentrate on more important matters. Why then did he feel he was missing something, and why did that make him feel sad when he should be deliriously happy?

The engaged couple sat in a horse-drawn carriage as it drove through the streets of the city. They both smiled and waved to the crowds who waved back, cheering them and offering their congratulations. Prince Michael even caught one or two lewd remarks of advice for his wedding night which he took with good grace. Then he caught a glimpse of a woman in the crowd hauntingly familiar. Though he only got a fleeting glance, somehow her beauty was etched in his head as if he had known her before. Amelia noticed the strange look in the prince's eyes.

"What is wrong, Michael, are you not feeling well? Should we return to the castle?"

The prince shook himself as if coming out of a trance and smiled at the princess, "No, it's nothing my dear... I just thought I saw someone I knew in the crowd, but I must have been mistaken."

The masked autumn ball was the last event before the planned wedding. Many guests attended the ball, including the aged King of Valantia who proudly accompanied his daughter. It was the first time King Marcus left his palace for some time; being in poor health. He did not want to miss this chance to show off his daughter before she wed Prince Michael. The wedding would cement both countries into one great country; a goal the king had worked for most of his life. The wedding would be his crowning achievement. He could finally retire knowing his daughter was in good hands. The two monarchs danced together and talked about the forthcoming wedding. The evening drew on, and the prince danced first with the princess, then they changed partners. Even though they were masked, the royal dress of both monarchs, and their respected offspring made it so they could not be mistaken for anyone else. It was the last dance of the evening, and Michael changed partners once again. Taking the lady by the hand, he found himself caught up in the dance. There was something about her; she seemed so poised and graceful, and her perfume overpowered his senses. He found himself wishing he could dance longer with her. As the dance ended, the lady briefly lowered her mask and smiled.

"Remember me," she said.

Something about the women and the words she spoke, '*Remember me,*' struck a chord with the prince. His head started to throb, and he suddenly felt dizzy; most of all, his heart ached so much as if a great weight pressed on it – the pain was almost unbearable. He staggered, holding a hand to his head. He looked for the woman, certain that she knew what was wrong with him, but she had vanished. Everyone stared at him with concern wondering if the malady they almost forgot about returned to plague the prince once more. The queen rushed to help the prince, removing her mask so that she could see more clearly what was wrong with her son.

A few days after the ball, King Marcus sat on the throne, his brow creased with worry his head resting on the palm of his hand. He looked up as the knight captain approached the throne.

The knight captain bowed, "Sire,"

"What news, Sir Derwin, has the prince recovered?"

"Yes, Sire, he has recovered enough, for now; the wedding will go ahead as planned."

The king sighed with relief and nodded, "Good, Good, all is well then."

"About that other matter you asked me to look into, Sire," the knight captain said.

"Yes, have you found anything yet?" The king scratched his chin, giving the knight captain a curious look.

"I believe the girl was not murdered as intended; she may yet live. The soldier who was supposed to kill her is dead now, but his wife lives still. I took the liberty of bringing her here; she awaits without, Sire," the knight captain said at length.

The king's eyes widened, and his hand trembled ever so slightly, "Show her in at once; I will question her myself."

The knight captain bowed, "At once, Sire." He turned and called for his men to show the woman in.

The king studied the woman carefully as she entered the throne room, accompanied by two soldiers. She was old with a weathered face and white hair; her dress was not too shabby and showed that she took some care in her appearance. She looked overwhelmed to be in the presence of the king.

She bowed several times, shaking, her eyes wide, her voice trembled as she spoke, "Your Majesty... I ... I'm honoured to be here. What is it you want from me?" she said apprehensively

The king was not unsympathetic as he regarded the woman, "Calm yourself, you're not in any trouble. I only want to ask you if you remember what happened to the girl your late husband was ordered to kill twenty years ago. You can be honest, I won't hold anything against you." The woman looked uncertain still. The king sighed,

"No harm will come to you if the girl was spared and lives. I simply wish to know was she killed or not. Nor do I wish to harm her if she is alive," the king explained at length.

The woman frowned, she kept looking down not at the king. Still shaking slightly, she sighed coming to a decision, "She lives, my Sam didn't have the heart to kill the poor girl. We hid her away at our home for a few days. When it was safe, we took to the forester's home."

The king nodded, digesting the information for a few moments, "The forester's home?"

"Yes, Your Majesty, we visited a few times for the first few years, and she seemed to be growing up well; eventually, we lost touch. I doubt that she will still there after all this time."

Again, the king nodded scratching his chin absently, "Very well. Before you go, I will say one thing to you now," the king paused his expression grave. "It's a little late, but I want to thank you both you and your husband for saving the girl. It was an evil deed my late wife planned. One which I nor anyone knowing the difference between right and wrong cannot forgive. The king paused again, sighing. "You may go now," he said finally. The king ordered the knight captain to see that the woman was fed first then given coin for her trouble before seeing her safely home.

Finale

Prince Michael stood nervously waiting for his bride to enter; he looked pale and gaunt ever since the night of the ball. He felt unwell and had several relapses. He kept seeing the same face in his dreams. The prince had never been able to get to the bottom of who the woman was and whether she was real or just a figment of his imagination. He wondered why it bothered him so much; putting such thoughts behind him, he smiled in anticipation of his forthcoming nuptials. King Marcus entered with his daughter on his arm. The princess smiled, looking enchanting in a dazzling full-length white gown with sequins. Music played as the king and the princess slowly walked up the aisle with two bridesmaids holding the bridal gown's train aloft. Finally, they mounted the few steps onto the podium. King Marcus left his daughter with her intended to sit on the right next to Queen Phoebe. The couple stood at last next to one and other. They smiled at each other like a devoted couple – the ceremony about to begin.

Suddenly, the enchantress appeared cloaked and hooded as usual startling everyone present! In one hand, she held the dagger she used previously when treating the prince the markings on the dagger clearly seen now of two hearts entwined. The prince suddenly fell ill, staggering; his face going deathly pale as before his head hurt his heart feeling heavy. As the enchantress strode up the aisle, ignoring the confusion around her. The guests startled tried to comprehend what was happening. Princess Amelia seeing the dagger in the enchantress's hand called out, "She has a dagger she aims to kill us," she pointed at the enchantress.

Queen Phoebe stood alarmed, her eyes going wide she struggled to gather her thoughts, "This all your fault enchantress you bewitched my son – look, he has fallen ill again now you are here," she shouted accusingly. " Stop her! Stop her now, I command it."

The enchantress stopped a moment her face rigid as she stared at the queen, "Not so, I tried my best to cure him I told you this would happen, and how-to completely cure him, but you ignored you my warning." The soldiers rushed to stop the enchantress, but all fell unconscious before getting anywhere near her as she continued up the aisle.

"But the princess is his one true is she not?" the king finally spoke out getting to his feet.

The enchantress shook her head slowly, "No, she is not," she began. "She is the one bewitching the prince with the concoctions she had brewed for her to make him forget and fall in love with her," the enchantress explained.

"No, that can't be she wouldn't not Amelia," the king said disbelievingly.

The enchantress finally stood on the podium facing the prince and the monarchs while the princess shrunk back, fearful of the enchantress's wrath. The enchantress pulled back her hood, revealing her face – the similarity between the enchantress and the princess could not go unnoticed for all there to see. "Yes, Father, I'm the daughter Mother tried to have killed... You now face the consequences!" She turned to face the princess, "Sister, your scheming led to the prince's malady in the first place... Consequences!" Then turning to Queen Phoebe. "You ignored my warning and insisted Amelia was the prince's, true love... Consequences!"

All went quiet and still in the great hall as they all listened enrapt in what the enchantress had to say. She held the dagger aloft more once, and a blinding light emitted from it, "Remember me," she said. Finally, the prince remembered. He remembered that he had known Melina since he was just a boy. Time and the princess's scheming made him forget until now, and he knew that Melina was his one true love.

A while later, the wedding took place as planned with one crucial change: Melina was the prince's bride. Shortly after the wedding princess, Amelia entered a secluded convent, king Marcus died of a broken heart, and Queen Phoebe stepped down as queen and was rarely seen again. Michael became king with Melina at his side as queen. An era of peace and prosperity began between the two countries now united as one. Two years later, a month after giving birth to her baby son, the mystic Nathanial came visiting.

Queen Melina smiled at seeing her old friend once more, "Nathan, my dear friend, it is good to see again."

The old mystic smiled looking at Melina sat cradling her child, "And you Melina," he said sighing.

Melina frowned, "Why the long sigh, Nathan?"

Nathan stared gravely at Queen Melina, "I have a warning for you...!"

The End

Winyd The Wolf: Wolf Dream

Winyd lay in a hole dug under a dead tree stump with just enough room to turn around. Ice crystals formed on his shaggy brown-grey fur. His breath steamed in the cold night air. Outside, the world was coloured white and grey as snow fell in a howling blizzard. Winyd dreamed in the way that wolves do and in this dream; he stood on a trail leading south. A great white wolf sat on its haunches in front of him barring his path

"You are going the wrong way you know," the white wolf said in the language of the wolves. Wolves tend to be pretty straightforward no-nonsense types when talking to one and other.

"Don't be silly," Winyd said. Sitting, he regarded the white wolf curiously. "Wolves from around here always go this way, to the lowlands in winter. It's less cold, and better hunting," his tongue lolling in what passed for laughter among wolves.

The white wolf spoke with an air most formal for a wolf. "That way lies death."

"I'd most likely die of starvation if I went into the mountains." Winyd, said not the least bit impressed by the white wolf's tone.

"Suit yourself, but if you go south you will be dead before winters end," the white wolf answered indifferently. Standing, he turned and ran northward his pace quickening as he blended in with the surroundings; until disappearing amongst the snow-clad trees.

As the sky lightened, to a grey and bleak dawn, Winyd awoke and scrambled from his make-shift lair; snow still fell but not as heavy as during the night. He shook himself to get the ice out of his fur and sniffed the air for any sign of danger, or possible prey. There was no scent of danger or prey – no sign of any life apart from the occasional bird. The forest in which Winyd stood, lay silent with only the wailing of the wind – blowing the snow into drifts which piled up against the trees and bushes.

Winyd bent his head and lapped up some snow, letting it melt in his mouth. Water wouldn't be a problem, but finding food would be. Winyd could remember past winters as worse as this one. However, this was already as bad as any he could remember, and all the signs indicated it would get worse. Winyd threaded his way through the undergrowth which had concealed his lair; dislodging snow from bushes, in passing. Out in the open, he sniffed the air again, his keen eyes searched the tree-lined forest for movement, but nothing stirred.

He shook himself again and headed in a southerly direction though he remembered his dream from the night before habit and instinct said he should travel south to the lowlands. Now wolves measure time, unlike men in hours and days, but by the rising of the moon and wolves could travel a long way in a day. In Winyd's estimate, it would typically take at least two or three risings of the moon to reach the lowlands but in present conditions. Winyd doubled his estimate and allowed himself four. He plodded along ever alert; ears pricked listening for the slightest sound. Hunger gnawed at him, but he had gone hungry before many times for long periods, he could endure it again. Around midday, after travelling none stop, he considered resting, for a while. The snow stopped; weak wintry sunlight shone through the trees; all of a sudden, Winyd heard a cracking noise. Instinctively, he turned on his fours and leapt just as a sizeable snow-laden branch came crashing to the ground barely missing him as it sprayed snow all around covering him, in a white powder. Winyd shook the snow from his fur and scrambled over the fallen branch. Deciding he had enough for one day, Winyd went in search of a place to spend the night.

Storm

The next day saw Winyd heading in the same direction, the forest thinned, and he would soon be in open country. The wind gusted through the trees blowing snow in eddies that occasionally rose to obscure the view ahead. It was afternoon when Winyd crested a low hill with stunted trees growing alongside mixed scrub bushes. He caught the scent of a familiar animal turning back he followed the scent keeping downwind as much as possible so that his prey couldn't detect him. He followed the smell, down a dip in the hillside, until he found the tell-tale tracks of a rabbit. He moved cautiously as the scent grew stronger, stalking his prey with patience and cunning. Realising this may be his last chance for some time to have anything to eat, he did not let the hunger he felt drive him to make a mistake, and alert the prey to his presence.

Occasionally, the wind turned to carry the scent away from him, and even the tracks would disappear blown by the wind. Then he stopped and waited until the scent came to him again in this way he followed until he finally glimpsed the rabbit close to its burrow. Winyd crouched low and stealthily crept up behind the rabbit. At the last moment, just as the rabbit caught his scent, he pounced his teeth sinking into the rabbit's neck. The rabbit struggled desperately to break free but, Winyd clenched his jaws tight, and soon the rabbit struggled no more.

The meat was lean but enough to stave back the hunger and replenish his strength. Winyd sat near the remains of his kill, cleaning himself when the scent of more wolves came to him. He stood ears pricked, watching as he saw three wolves ghosting out of the forest; they soon caught his scent and approached warily. Winyd recognised the pack leader, a she-wolf whom he had hunted with, in past seasons Storm was her name he remembered, she came with two males in tow and stood to face him. She was smaller and her fur a lighter colour than most wolves who dwelled in the mountains

"You got a kill I see, Winyd,' Storm said in a weary tone.

"You are welcome to what's left Storm, though it could have been more if you had come sooner." He knew there wasn't much left worth having, and he didn't have to give them anything he wasn't of their pack. Winyd liked Storm, they hunted well together in the past as she-wolves go, she was everything a male wolf could wish for.

"You are kind to offer even though there is little left Winyd," Storm answered. The two male wolves didn't look too pleased, but Storm ignored them as she nibbled at the rabbit remains before snagging it in her jaws and flinging it towards her pack mates. The two hungrily tore apart what remained of the rabbit

Winyd had been feeling uneasy since he dreamed of the white wolf and thought he could confide in Storm about his dream. When he finished telling her, she looked curiously at him before speaking. "I have heard tell of the great white wolf, it is said, he is the father and protector of all wolves," Storm said after some thought. "If he came to you in a dream to warn you, I wouldn't take it lightly. Though it is strange indeed for as you say to go back into the mountains would seem foolish," she continued at length. "What shall you do, Winyd?" She asked as her two pack mates finished the remains of the rabbit and waited expectantly.

"I have never heard of the father of all wolves before," Winyd began. "As to what I'll do, if you permit, I would like to travel with your pack a while and think on what you said," Winyd said in conclusion.

"You are welcome, Winyd," She answered with what passed for a smile among wolves.

They spent the night under some bushes and moved on at daybreak. The sky turned a steel grey, and no sun shone through the clouds. It felt even colder than the day before, Winyd's uneasiness remained. When they reached the river, he knew he needed to decide whether to go on or turn back. Strictly speaking, he didn't have to go back; yet, he could keep on this side of the river and follow it westerly before turning north if he decided to do what the white wolf told him. When he gave that idea some thought, it seemed to fit, and his uneasiness subsided.

River Parting

The river had frozen over although there were places the ice appeared to be thin and cracked where a trickle of water flowed still; crossing would not be as easy as it seemed. Winyd left Storm, deciding not to cross with her and the other wolves. He saw them get safely across though not without some difficulty. Winyd followed the river westward as far as he could before turning north again. Snow fell once more, the air still as Winyd struggled through deep snowdrifts. Travelling upwards across a ridge lined with pine trees then down into a gulley, he detected no movement anywhere. Snow fell steadily, becoming heavier as the day wore on. The moon rose in the sky again, as Winyd finally found a place to shelter in a hollow. Far away in the distance, to the south, he heard a noise carried on the still air. Two, three times or more, he listened to the same sound. He wondered what it might be as he curled up and drifted into a deep sleep. He dreamt, and the white wolf appeared again in his dream this time on a mountaintop.

"I've done what you said. Now I'm sure to die before winter is over," Winyd said resigned to his fate.

"You are not dead yet are you?" The white wolf stated succinctly. "There is a valley no further than two risings of the moon. Make it that far, and we will speak again," said the white wolf. Winyd woke covered in snow, he dug himself out and shook the snow from his fur. The day was bright, clear and bitter cold. Winyd managed to dig out some grubs and one or two nuts from under the pine trees. Though meagre, they were enough to sustain him a while. He travelled onward climbing higher into an unknown mountainous landscape, with snow-covered fir and pine trees. He managed to find a hollowed tree trunk to sleep in as it grew dark. The moon rose, bright in the night sky. The next morning, colder still with icicles hanging from the trees. The snow crisp and hard underfoot. Winyd struggled to get himself moving, slipping and sliding, but he managed to keep going. At midday, the sky turned a dark, ominous grey, and it began to snow. First, a little then eventually in a howling windswept blizzard. Winyd couldn't see beyond his nose instinct and the sheer will to survive kept will going.

The White Wolf Speaks

As the moon rose once again, Winyd could go no further exhausted he lay in the snow. "You are giving up then I see," said the white wolf. Winyd wondered if he was dreaming again, but this time he wasn't. The white wolf sat on his haunches nearby watching him.

"It's too late for me, I told you I would die if I went this way," Winyd said philosophically.

"But you are not dead yet, time to get moving," answered the white wolf. Winyd forced himself up to stand on all fours his legs shaking with the effort. The white wolf ran onward vanishing he called to Winyd, "Not much further now then you can rest."

Winyd followed the white wolf; every time he got near to him, he would vanish and reappear further ahead. Finally, he stopped in front of what appeared to be a low overhanging rock face. When Winyd reached the overhang, he crouched down and scrambled under it. To his surprise, it opened up into a small cave not very high, but enough so he could stand upright. Inside, it widened out a little and went deeper into the rock face. He could hear and smell rats scurrying about. He lay still and waiting patiently; eventually, several rats came. He pounced, killing two before the rest ran off, disappearing into the darkness. The rats were lean but with enough meat to help regain his strength. The cave though still cold, was warmer than outside and gave shelter from the elements.

Winyd slept and dreamed; he stood in a broad valley. The white wolf sat next to him. "You must save the one that awaits in the valley below if you are to survive the winter." The white wolf said cryptically.

"Who must I save, " Winyd asked remembering, Storm and hoped it might be she that awaited him in the valley.

"It is not she," the white wolf said. Reading his thoughts, "She yet lives, though."

"Then who," pressed Winyd

"You will see, but if you fail to save the one that awaits. You both will die and, ultimately, Storm before winter's end. It will be your hardest test yet," said the white wolf enigmatically.

Winyd woke and caught another rat and a few insects that lived in the cave. He rested another day until finally feeling back to full strength before he ventured out. The day was bright and sunny, but there was no warmth in the sun. A biting wind blew across the frozen landscape. The wind lessened the air feeling a little less cold as he headed down into a valley. He came across tracks and caught the scent of a bear, although faint now a bear recently passed here. He continued his descent into the valley floor. Giant fir, pine, and spruce trees grew all around. The valley long and narrow with occasional rising slopes and dips. The sun low in the sky when he saw smoke rising above the trees just beyond a rise. Winyd knew what the smoke meant. He wanted to turn around and avoid the area the smoke came from, but something drove him towards it. He topped the rise, entering a clearing, ahead was a man lair; men called them by several names which were confusing to a wolf. He had seen many such places before in the lowlands. Winyd stopped crouching down he watched intently uncertain what he should do.

The Man

He caught the scent of a bear again; it came shambling out of the trees near to the man's lair. Still crouched Winyd hurridly crept nearer and nearer. He caught the scent of the man as he came out of his den carrying one of the long sticks that spurted fire and death. Instinctively Winyd knew this was the moment the white wolf told him off. However, he wasn't sure whom he should try and save both were dangerous to him. The bear, driven by hunger and the need to survive saw the man as a rival predator and a source of food. The man could have many reasons, including those of the bear. As Winyd considered what to do, the man fired his long stick at the bear as it rushed towards him. The bear stumbled to one side momentary losing momentum, but continued its charge.

Instinctively, Winyd went for the bear attacking it's hind legs while still charging the man. The bear stopped half turned it swung one massive paw at Winyd. He yelled in pain and went spinning in the snow. The man fired again still the bear kept on as the man stumbled. Winyd was up; blood oozed from his side. Once again, he attacked this time he lept on to the bear's back as the man managed to get to his feet. He sank his teeth into the bear's neck, locking his jaw tight and held on as the bear swung wildly trying to shake him off. The man backed away reloaded and fired again. The bear roared in pain and rage, Winyd finally released his grip on the bear spitting fur and skin from his mouth. A deep gouged wound streamed blood, where Winyd had sunk his teeth into the neck of the bear. He jumped as the bear took a stumbling step forward. Winyd backed away from the bear as it fell catching a glancing blow as the bear thrashed about in its death throes. Winyd rolled sideways yelling in pain, unable to move his whole body ached; the pain from his wounded side unbearable. The man stood over him with the long stick pointed at him. Winyd considered he may have chosen wrong now he would die.

Then all was darkness!

Winyd awoke to find himself in the man's lair. He lay close to a fire he had seen fire before, but never been this close it warmed him and felt good. There were many smells, some new and strange, some familiar. The dominating scent was that of the man who sat nearby watching him. He could sense the man was wary of him, and he felt the same as the man. There was food next to him, so he ate and drank; the food was a new taste to him and strange at first, but he ate it all then slept.

He awakened, feeling a little stronger; the man tended his wounds while he slept. Winyd struggled to his feet; there was no sign of the man, and there seemed no way of getting out he felt trapped. He decided to investigate the man's lair wandering around sniffing at different things. Suddenly, the entrance opened and the man entered; seeing Winyd wasn't by the fire, he quickly scanned around until he spotted Winyd. Still wary of one and other, the man stepped away from the entrance. Letting Winyd out to relieve himself on returning, he found the door closed. He scraped at it with his paws until the man came and let him in again. Winyd laid once more by the fire and dreamed. The white wolf sat next to him by the fire.

"Man's fire is good is it not?" the white wolf said.

"Yes, it feels good as long as you don't touch it," replied Winyd. He was lost in thought a moment as the white wolf scrutinised him carefully expecting more. "Why did you bring me here?" Winyd finally asked.

"Why to save you for you are the last of the mountain wolves, and the first," answered the white wolf in his usual enigmatic way.

"If I am the last, then my kind will be no more," said Winyd, gloomily.

"You do not understand yet," the white wolf began. "Heed my words, you can trust this man but no other for now," said the white wolf. He vanished, and Winyd awakened in the comfort of the man's lair.

Winter's End

Slowly, the man and Winyd began to trust each other and develop a deep bond. They enjoyed each others company as the long winter days and nights drew out. Food was in short supply for both of them. They hunted together, catching whatever they could find to survive. It was a hard existence, but Winyd didn't mind he was alive, and the man seemed to feel the same. Several times, the weather was too bad to go out and they stayed inside. Then one day, the snow showed signs of melting – the air fresh though still cold. The valley showed signs of life returning buds appeared on the trees and tufts of grass thrust upwards out of the snow.

It was on such a day that more men appeared. Winyd and the man were relaxing, taking in the midday sun; its warmth felt good after the long, harsh winter. Winyd caught their scent long before they arrived. With a low growl that surprised them, he took off and hid amongst the trees where he could watch the men approach without being seen. Instinct told him these men were not like the man whom he considered a packmate; they were a danger to him at least. They would not understand a wolf living alongside a man and could even prove a danger to the man if they knew. He watched from his hiding place – hackles raised, ears pricked – he wondered if the man would tell them about him. They talked in the man tongue then went to the man's lair and exchanged some goods before leaving again. The man looked around for him after they had gone from sight. Winyd came out of hiding still wary; he could see and sense from the man he felt the same. The man bent down and ran his hand through Winyd's fur in a way that seemed to please both of them.

Some days later, Winyd while out hunting with the man he caught the scent of another wolf, but he also had a sense that this wolf was in trouble. He stopped in his tracks, ears pricked; he sniffed the air for any sound. Suddenly, another wolf sprang out between the trees panting hard.

"Storm," Winyd said.

Storm had been running hard to escape the men chasing her, and reckless in what may lay ahead though she caught the scent of another wolf close. Storm came to a halt suddenly seeing the man. Thinking herself trapped, she was about to make a last desperate effort and attack the man.

"Stop!" Winyd began," seeing Storm was about to attack. "He is my packmate, we can help you escape," Winyd said.

Storm hesitated in a state of confusion and panic the idea of a man being Winyd's packmate was alien to her. But Winyd had survived here through the worst winter she could remember when she gave it some thought with the help of a man it would seem more likely.

"Fine, Winyd, I trust you, but other men are chasing; how do we get away from them?" asked Storm.

The man watched the two wolves intently and got the impression they knew each other. The other, he surmised, was female so he assumed she was friendly. He waved his hand about and pointed back towards his lair. Winyd having picked up many of the man's hand movements though he didn't understand fully. He got the gist of what they meant: run and hide! So, calling to Storm, they both ran.

The man met the pursuers; they spoke awhile, giving the two wolves more time to get away. He indicated, pointing in a different direction to where the wolves had gone. The men nodded going in the direction he suggested. Walking back, he saw the two wolves together; smiling, he shook his head, wondering what he was going to do with two wolves.

A New Beginning

Winyd slept with Storm at his side; the white wolf appeared to both of them. He guided both to this point, and now he would speak to them for one last time. It would be up to themselves from this point on.

"You are not dead, either of you, I see," said the white wolf.

"Thanks to you," Storm said.

"I still don't understand all of what you told me," Winyd said, looking curiously at the white wolf.

"What part did you not understand," the white wolf replied.

"You said I was the last of my kind, yet I am not for Storm is here," said Winyd curiously.

"Oh, but Storm is truly not of the mountain wolf, so therefore you are the last of your kind for now," answered the white wolf in an amused tone.

It was a warm summer's day when the two wolves set off on their way running and jumping in the long grass – chasing one and other amid the trees until they disappeared from view. The man watched them go; he would not see them again till winter returned then there would be more mouths to feed.

The End

Ellie and the Fire Demon

It all began one beautiful summer's day. At five years of age, Ellie was a bright child with blonde curly hair and blue eyes. Her parents were very proud of her and loved her dearly. Anyone who met Ellie was instantly enchanted by her friendly and caring nature. She was always well-behaved and never bad-tempered.

Her parents had chartered a light aircraft to go on a business trip. They considered leaving Ellie with her grandparents, but she wanted to go with them. So they relented and made arrangements for Ellie to travel with them. It was Ellie's first time away from home and her first time flying. She was very excited about it. Her parents had fretted about how Ellie would react to air travel, but as usual, Ellie took it all in her stride.

Her father took Ellie to the pilot, who explained all about the different instruments and dials. He even let her take control of the aeroplane for a moment or two. However, it was all a little too technical for Ellie to grasp. Ellie looked out of the cockpit window at the dark clouds looming ahead. Something about the clouds made her suddenly go cold and very frightened.

Ellie tried to tell the pilot that they ought to go around the clouds, that something terrible would happen if they didn't. The pilot told her not to worry, it was the just bad weather. They would be out of it in no time and told everyone to sit and fasten their seatbelts. Ellie became frantic. She asked her parents to make the pilot turn back.

Ellie's parent's tried to reassure her that it would be fine. They would be out of the clouds soon and be landing shortly.

All the time, the clouds grew nearer and darker, flashes of lightning could be seen within. Turbulence buffeted the plane, making it rise and fall and tilt left and right erratically. Then they were in the dark clouds. Even Ellie's parents became a little worried, but tried not to show their anxieties lest they upset Ellie more than she already was.

Ellie bit her lip terror-stricken she had exhausted her herself shouting and begging the pilot to turn back. She could do no more but wait for what she believed would be inevitable.

Lightning struck the plane!

Everything seemed to happen at once. The plane was falling, and one of the engines caught fire. Miraculously, Ellie survived the crash with just minor injuries. The newspapers called Ellie the miracle child. But the once bright girl became melancholy and withdrawn. Ellie kept insisting a fire demon had taken her parents and the pilot. Everyone spoke kindly to her. Telling her not to worry – there were no such things as fire demons – and spoke sympathetically to her. In the meantime, Ellie went to live with her grandparents after recovering from her injuries in hospital. The doctors, whom Ellie's grandparents had taken her to see, all said the same thing. The fire demon was just Ellie's way of dealing with the trauma of the crash and the loss of her parents.

Years passed and Ellie once more became a bright and happy child. Though there remained a touch of sadness about her that made everyone think she hadn't quite gotten over the plane crash. Ellie's grandmother took her to school in her car every weekday, where Ellie had made many friends. At the weekends, her grandparents would often take Ellie for a drive in the countryside or even to the seaside. Ellie loved the water and could swim like a fish, according to her grandfather. Ellie's favourite place, when at the beach, was an island a short distance from the mainland where seabirds liked to nest; to Ellie, it was so peaceful. She felt safe and secure there away from the troubles and cares of ordinary life.

Late one warm summer's night, Ellie awoke from a deep sleep. She lay wondering what had awakened her. The air was still and stifling… then she heard a sound that terrified her. It brought back vague and disturbing memories from years past. Somehow, Ellie knew she must get out of the house. Quickly putting on her dressing gown, she went to her grandparent's room. Ellie couldn't explain why, she just knew they had to get out of the house. So she just shook them awake, telling them the house was on fire.

Her grandparents woke confused. They had no reason to doubt Ellie even though there seemed to be no sign of any fire. They hurriedly dressed, and her grandfather phoned the fire brigade before they all rushed into the street. But everything seemed normal; no fire or smoke was coming from the house. Ellie's grandfather was about to protest with Ellie about raising a false alarm when, suddenly, a bolt of lightning hit the home. Flames quickly spread by the time the fire brigade arrived – the house was well ablaze. Ellie stood, watching the flames. She could hear the hateful crackling of the fire, almost like laughter, but she had escaped once more.

After the fire, Ellie's grandparents decided to move nearer the sea. So with the help of the insurance money they collected on their old house, they moved to the seaside where they often visited. Ellie was thrilled, for it meant she could visit her favourite place: the island she called her own. She could even go swimming every day! Unfortunately for her, she had to start over again at a different school and found making new friends not as easy.

Ellie made one friend though Susan. Susan's parents moved into the area shortly after Ellie had, and the two quickly became friends. On Ellie's eleventh birthday, her grandparents invited Susan to her birthday party. It was a grand party with jelly, ice-cream sandwiches and all sorts of fancy cakes. Ellie had never felt happier since the loss of her parents. As she sat looking at the faces of her grandparents and her friend, she felt a dark shadow was hanging over them.

One day shortly after her birthday, Ellie and Susan were walking home from school when Ellie heard that sound again: the sound from before that filled her with terror. She shouted to Susan to run as fast as she could, but Susan stood wondering what was wrong for only Ellie could hear the sound, that horrible crackling laughter of the fire demon. Everything seemed usual; it was a bright sunny day and there was no cause for any concern. So Ellie grabbed Susan by the hand and started running, dragging her along.

"You have to try and run faster than me," Ellie said, making it sound as if it was to be a race. Susan nodded understanding at last. Both girls ran as fast as they could. By the time they reached Susan's house, Ellie no longer could hear the dreadful sound. Susan waved goodbye, saying the race had been good fun and they should do it again sometime. Ellie hoped as she walked the rest of the way home, if they were to race again, it wouldn't be in quite the same circumstances.

The next day, the newspapers reported some strange events – lightning striking several trees in one area, and a peculiar fire where someone was seriously injured. Ellie told her grandparents the fire demon had come again and was trying to get her, although they didn't believe her about the fire demon since the incident when lightning struck the house. They had a healthy respect for what they thought were Ellie's premonitions, so they told her to let them know if she had any more warnings. Ellie assured her grandparents she would.

"I won't let anything bad happen to you and Grandpa, or Susan," Ellie assured her grandmother so fiercely. Her grandmother hugged Ellie and kissed her on the forehead. As she let her go, she brushed an unshed tear from her eye

"I know, dear; I know you won't," her grandmother replied, her voice husky with emotion.

Ellie's grandparents became very watchful of Ellie. They would take her to school each day even though the school was only a short distance away. One of them would be there early to pick her up when school ended. Ellie still played with Susan and confided in her about the fire demon. Susan didn't believe Ellie and thought she was making it up. Ellie was not put off by the fact Susan nor her grandparents believed her and knew one day the fire demon would return.

All returned to normal until just before Ellie's thirteenth birthday. Ellie realised that the fire demon always came around at a particular time of year. If it were to come again, now would be the time. It was a sunny, warm day; the sky was a deep azure blue. Broken only by a few fluffy white clouds, a slight breeze came from the sea. Ellie and her grandparents were at the beech. People sat on deck chairs or lying on the sands sunbathing. Children played with bucket and spade making sandcastles, while others paddled or swam in the sea; a few played beach ball or catch.

Ellie sat on the sand, watching the sea while her grandparents sat nearby on deck chairs. Her grandmother was knitting, and her grandfather read the daily newspaper. From where she sat, Ellie could see her favourite place it had been some time since she had been there. Ellie was lost in thought when she heard that sound again, though she felt dread it no longer frightened her as much as it used too. Ellie stood and walked bare-footed to her grandparents

"It's coming for me, but I won't let it get you as well," Ellie said with such a sad expression that it nearly broke the hearts of her grandparents.

They looked at each other then at Ellie and asked her what she meant. It was then that a commotion broke out further up the beach like someone starting several fires at once. As Ellie's grandparents stood to see what was happening, Ellie started running towards the sea. Ellie's grandparents watched in dismay as Ellie ran followed by what looked like jets of flame spouting from the sand. Ellie reached the sea and began swimming as hard as she could towards her favourite place. She had never swum the distance before but believed she could make it. Behind her, the water steamed and boiled. As she got nearer the island, the boiling water began to subside, and the sea was at last calm again.

Too far to turn back now, Ellie swam on; her arms ached and she could hardly breathe. She turned to take one last look back to see her grandparents frantically calling for help, before swimming on.

Home now, she thought, thrusting her arms out one last time as the island drew near. She could see her parents standing on the sandy shore waving and calling to her. She heard the seabirds that nestled amongst the craggy rocks and the splash of waves upon the shore. No more did she fear the fire demon; no more would the demon chase her. She was home and safe at last.

So if you ever go to the seaside and there is a little island just off the shore where seabirds nest. If ever you visit that island, maybe you will see Ellie playing on the beach or running between the rocks.

The End

The Coffee Shop

The sign outside the shop read, 'The Coffee Shop'. It was a small cafe situated in a large shopping mall with a quaint Victorian-style look, right down to having china cups and crockery. It stood out from other cafes and restaurants within the mall. A friendly waitress would bring your order to you and it was very popular with shoppers.

Shortly after Easter on a busy lunchtime, Lucy and Anne sat having coffee. Lucy had her usual latte while Anne preferred a cappuccino. The two had become friends since they started working together in the large department store close to the coffee shop. They often had their lunch break in The Coffee Shop. It had a warm homely atmosphere. Lucy was nearly ten years, Anne's senior and in her late forties. She took Anne under her wing ever since Anne started as a new girl over a year ago.

Anne was busy talking about her new boyfriend; Lucy hardly heard her as she glanced over at the man sat opposite a few tables up. She guessed his age at around the late fifties, early sixties. He appeared average in height with short silver hair, dressed casually, and always neat and tidy. As usual, he carried a bag filled with shopping, so she deduced he more than likely lived alone.

"Not him again," Anne finally said seeing Lucy wasn't listening to her.

"I can't help it, I think that he is so handsome," Lucy replied sighing.

"But he must be really old," Anne said.

Lucy turned sharply to face Anne, frowning. "I'm no spring chicken myself now, and age is only a number, right?" Lucy said, looking across once more at the man.

He suddenly looked up and caught her staring then turned back to his almost-finished latte. Lucy had known quite a few men in her life, but never got close to any. Never had she been in bed with a man. She turned one or two down flat, and nearly done the deed with another, thinking him to be the one until finding out he was dating another woman at the same time. *"What a lucky escape that had been."* Now Lucy wondered if she should have been less picky and jumped in the sack with one or two of the men she had known, in the past. It may have worked. One of them might have been her Mr Right for all she knew.

"Well, if that's what you think, why don't you go and talk to him," Anne said, not sounding if she really meant it.

Lucy was considering doing just that. He was so handsome that when she looked at him, she went all shaky and felt a queasiness in her stomach. Suddenly, Lucy felt flushed and needed the loo. "I'm just going to the toilet. Maybe I'll go talk to him after," Lucy said standing. Anne nodded as Lucy turned, walking to the back of the cafe. As she passed the man, she glanced down at him, but he paid no attention to her. When she returned, he was gone. *"Well, maybe next time,"* Lucy sighed to herself, sitting to finish her coffee.

The following week, Lucy and Anne were sitting in their usual seats; there was no sign of the man as yet. *"Maybe he won't come this week,"* Lucy mused, but then Anne leaned across and poked her arm and indicated by nodding her head looking over Lucy's shoulder. Lucy sat with her back to the door, so didn't see him enter. She heard him order his usual latte with a scone, his voice having a mellow tone to her ears.

"You know, maybe he is just lonely and could do with someone to talk to," said Lucy.

"Well, you know what I said before go and talk to him," said Anne dismissively, while busy texting her boyfriend. She didn't think Lucy would do it. All she ever did was talk about it and never actually went and talked to the man. So she was shocked when Lucy stood up to do just that.

"Lucy! I wasn't serious," Anne exclaimed too loudly.

"Well I am," Lucy retorted just as loud. Everyone in the cafe turned to see where the commotion was coming from, including Lucy's intended target. Lucy picked up her latte and strode to where he sat. Her heart beat faster and faster until she thought it might burst out of her chest. Lucy never experienced anything like this before; she usually had no trouble talking to men, but this was something else. She felt confused, but managed to calm herself as she neared his table.

Tom looked up to see who caused the commotion. The two ladies who came here most weeks seemed to be having some disagreement. He knew by the name badges they wore that they worked in the department store nearby. He gathered that they were often here for their lunch break. Both women were beautiful, he thought. One was quite a few years younger than the other. He liked the older one the most; she seemed to have a kind face and a confident manner about her. Both of course too young for him. *"A pity,"* he thought with a sigh. He was startled when the older lady came towards him carrying her coffee. She had shoulder-length jet black hair and wore a light brown jacket and a blue skirt with black stiletto shoes that made her an inch or two taller. Only now, at close quarters, did he realise how attractive she appeared to him, bringing a flush to his cheeks. He wanted to get up and leave, but felt trapped. Suddenly leaving now would only make his embarrassment worse.

"Do you mind if I sit next to you?" she asked, her voice calm and collected she was relieved to note. When he didn't respond immediately, she continued. "I've had a tiff with my friend over there, and I don't want to sit alone." Noticing there were nearby empty tables she needed more of an excuse to sit next to him. She looked over her shoulder at Anne who was staring across at them, and gave her an angry look. Anne looked bemused, shrugged her shoulders and looked away. Lucy sat down, not waiting for his answer.

"I had noticed that," Tom said with a slight smile trying to make light of the situation to cover his embarrassment.

He was blushing, Lucy thought, a full-grown man of his age, blushing how charming. Lucy gave her best reassuring smile, sipped her coffee and leaned over a little towards him, staring into his deep blue eyes and asked his name.

"Tom," he replied. "And you are Lucy," he added, indicating to her badge. "Everybody in the cafe heard your little spat! You're famous now," he said. Despite the calmness of his voice, inside he was shaking. *You stupid old fool, she must be nearly twenty years younger, what would such a woman want with me? She either feels sorry for me or is just playing games.*

"A good sense of humour too," Lucy hadn't meant to say that out loud; she leaned further over towards him. He had one hand on the table, and she felt compelled to grasp his hand in hers. A shock shivered through her as their hands were briefly together.

Frowning, he pulled away from her. They finished their coffee in silence then unexpectedly he stood. Looking directly at her, he spoke quietly, "Look, as much as I'm flattered by your attention, shouldn't a beautiful woman like you be looking for someone nearer your age? Don't say age is just a number. I wish I had a pound for every time I've heard that line." The words seemed harsher than intended; he turned to leave.

Lucy felt shaken to the core that he would shun her in such a manner and angry too. "That's what you think," her bottom lip trembling with the shock of his rejection. Maybe she had been a bit to forward on reflection. Yes, she had, but there was no need for that tone. She felt devastated. Lucy stood and returned to Anne, who was looking at Lucy with some concern. Anne thought Lucy was close to tears. Muttering under her breath, Anne turned and scowled at the man.

Tom realised too late he had overstepped the mark and hurt Lucy. *What a fool I am, but it's probably for the best anyway.* Turning, he walked over to their table. Anne kept scowling angrily at him. Tom considered, he better at least apologise to Lucy.

"Look, I'm sorry, Lucy; I was wrong to speak as I did and assumimg to know what's best for you when I hardly know you," he said with sincerity.

Lucy could tell he genuinely regretted what he said and that he upset her; she could see it in his eyes. The rejection still hurt, so she turned away and didn't answer him. Anne, however, had a few choice words for him.

Over the following two weeks, there was no sign of Tom in the cafe. Lucy asked the manager if she had seen him. Perhaps he had been in when they weren't, but nobody had seen him. Anne told her to forget him, but Lucy had seen that look of regret in his eyes. *What was it about men with that wounded puppy dog look that made women want to hold them close to comfort and reassure them that all will be well? Wasn't it supposed to be the man's job to reassure the woman? Then again, maybe it worked both ways.* Lucy decided that maybe it didn't matter. Either way, he was so handsome she felt drawn to him like a moth to a flame. She still remembered when she held his hand in hers; the sensation had sent a warm tingling down her arm that was almost sensual. *Well maybe that was an overreaction. I liked touching him; anyway, it felt good and right.* She paused for a moment before continuing her train of thought. *Damn, I think I'm falling for him and I hardly know him! How ridiculous is that!*

On Friday – on the third week since their disasterous interaction – and with their lunch break nearly half over, Lucy sat facing the door, so she could see Tom when he walked in. He glanced around the cafe and, seeing Anne and Lucy, he hesitated. Lucy thought he might turn around and walk out again. He seemed to gather himself and order his usual latte, but with a slice of cheesecake this time. She only now realised that he liked some of the same things she did: lattes, scones and cheesecake were some of her favourites as well. He glanced at them, but didn't speak as he walked past and found a spare table at the back of the room. Lucy waited while the waitress brought his coffee and cheesecake. Then she stood to go to him. Anne looked at her, shaking her head. "Go on then, but if he says one wrong word to you, he'll have me to answer to," Anne said with venom in her voice that it surprised Lucy.

"Thanks, Anne, you are a good friend. I might be a bit late back to work, can you cover for me?"

"Sure thing, Lucy! Good luck, but remember, let me know if he upsets you again and I'll punch his lights out," Anne answered with a giggle as she waved Lucy off.

Tom looked up from his coffee as he heard footsteps approach; he knew who it would be even before looking up. They both spoke at the same time. "I want to apologise again," he began.

"We got off on the wrong foot," she started to say. Then they both paused. Tom waited for Lucy to speak first; they both smiled at one and other.

"Look, Tom, I know you think I'm too young for you, but can't we at least just be friends? I like you. I'm not asking for anything else. I have no ulterior motive; I find you an interesting man," she said, biting her bottom lip as she waited for his answer. *Well, maybe I do have an ulterior motive, what am I doing! Maybe he is right, what do I hope would come of the two of us just being friends. Oh damn, just wing it and see where it goes,* she thought – giving up trying to reason with herself.

He seemed to consider her words for what seemed like an eternity. His expression was serious like someone weighing the odds of a critical decision. Finally, his mood lightened as his eyes met hers. "Fair enough, I also find you to be an interesting person. I can't see any harm in us being friends, and I've missed female company."

Lucy realised she had been holding her breath while waiting for his answer. She let it go as she finally sat down; she didn't dare sit before. She was not going to push things, just be grateful for what she had. He did not, could not, know how she felt about him; she felt sure now that she was falling in love with him – maybe she had been from the first time she set eyes on him. Insane as that sounded to her, she knew he would only consider her as a friend now, but maybe in time that would change. Lucy had to hope and be patient. *What was that he said… missing female company?* she considered this snippet of information a moment. *He was married before? Well, obviously, but he wore no wedding ring* Lucy deduced; he didn't seem like the divorcing kind. Leastways, she wanted to believe that of him and the way he had said it. *His wife must have died. Maybe that was it?* She didn't speak of that, though, remembering something he said on their unfortunate first encounter.

"By the way, thank you for the compliment when last we spoke," she said; he looked at her enquiringly. "A beautiful woman," she said, smiling. "You called me a beautiful woman, remember?" A hint of redness came and went to his cheeks as he managed to control his embarrassment.

"You have a good memory, though I'd sooner forget the last time," he said wincing slightly. "Apart from that part, which I meant, and which I'll say again: you are a beautiful woman."

Lucy positively felt herself glowing with the compliment. *Oh, he is such a charmer when he wants to be.* She relished the prospect of further meetings like this with him, but for now, she had to get back to work.

"So how did it go?" Anne asked, excitedly wanting to know everything that they talked about and took place between them. "Well," Anne tried again when Lucy didn't answer and seemed distracted.

"Well what?" Lucy finally asked with a faraway look.

"Wait, he didn't say something to upset you again?" asked Anne, her voice going up an octave.

"What no, no, keep your voice down," began Lucy. "He was a perfect gentleman and very charming," explained Lucy. Anne was about to say something, but suddenly stopped a sudden realisation came to her.

"OMG! OMG! You have fallen for him, haven't you?! I mean, you're really in love with him," Anne explained. This time, she held her voice low so only the two of them could hear.

"Took you long enough to figure it out," said Lucy smiling.

"But–" Anne started to say before Lucy interrupted

"He is so old," Lucy finished assuming what Anne was about to say. "Well, not to me he isn't," Lucy stated.

"Well, yes, I mean no! What I mean to say is you hardly know him, and you're in love with him. How long have you known?" Anne asked, getting confused, as this was a lot to take in. She couldn't believe she hadn't spotted the signs before.

"Almost from the first time I set eyes on him, though I didn't realise it straight away. Now, after today, I'm as certain as I can be," Lucy paused. "He thinks of me as a friend, so don't say anything to him when we meet in the future. I mean it, Anne! If you even give away a hint of how I feel about him, even accidentally, and scare him off I might never see him again," Lucy pleaded, making Anne promise not to reveal Lucy's true feelings for Tom, to anyone; it was to be their secret.

Weeks went by with Lucy and Tom regularly meeting and often sitting together in deep conversation. Even Anne was growing to like him, though she still thought he was a bit old for Lucy.

"I have a nice garden which I spend a lot of spare time in during the summer," Tom said as they sat talking.

"Oh, I do like flowers; maybe I can see your garden sometime," Lucy replied hopefully.

"Well, maybe or I can bring some photos of the garden for you to see," Tom answered, not quite saying yes or no.

Lucy took it as a maybe, and it would be good to see how good a gardener Tom was. She liked flowers and gardening, although she didn't have a garden herself. Lucy always wanted a garden of her own. She considered whether seeing his garden, or even just photos of it, would give her more insight into his character and at least a small step closer to him.

Later that week, the two sat together having a coffee and Tom brought some photos of his garden. Lucy was impressed. Tom had a lovely garden with so many flowers and colours; it was so neatly kept, she could tell that Tom had put a lot of hard work, love and care into the garden.

"Oh, it's so lovely, Tom. So many beautiful flowers; how I'd love to have a garden like that," Lucy said, looking through the photos. "Thank you for letting me see your photos," Lucy concluded with heartfelt sincerity. She was halfway reaching for his hand again and caught herself just in time.

Tom appeared not to notice Lucy withdrawing her hand; he was a little taken aback by such warm praise.

"Well, it's not that good; I've seen better," he said modestly, though still quietly pleased that she liked his garden so much. She seemed to understand the time and work he put into it.

The following week, they sat together and Anne joined them for a while before leaving early to meet her boyfriend.

"Is it getting serious with Anne and her boyfriend?" Tom enquired as he watched Anne rush out.

"Seems that way, but you never know with Anne. She has had more boyfriends than I've had hot dinners," said Lucy and they both laughed.

The following week as Tom sat with Lucy and Anne, he noticed that Lucy did not seem quite herself and was a little pale. "Are you keeping well, Lucy? You don't seem yourself today," Tom asked with concern.

Lucy gave a reassuring smile that made Tom feel at ease once more. "I'm fine, Tom, just a little under the weather. I'll be fine tomorrow," Lucy said brightly.

"It's not, err… a sort of a woman's problem?" Tom enquired with a slight flush of embarrassment. Anne giggled at this and Lucy gave her an elbow in the arm.

"Ouch," Anne retorted. "Serves you right, Anne, for embarrassing Tom that way," Lucy said. "No, Tom, it's nothing like that, and thank you for your concern; you are such a dear for worrying about me," Lucy concluded.

The next few weeks went by; Tom noticed that Lucy still looked a little pale. It was midsummer when he entered the cafe as usual and saw Lucy and Anne sat together; they didn't seem to notice him at first and were in a serious conversation with occasionally raised voices that he could catch snippets of what they were saying.

"You have to tell…" Anne was saying.

Lucy shook her head, "… better not say anything either," replied Lucy.

Anne sighed and nodded her head in agreement, but didn't look happy. The manager coughed loudly, and Lucy and Anne turned to see Tom; Lucy smiled, beckoning him to join them.

Tom wondered what was going on. The conversation seemed a little muted than usual; he was beginning to think of the worst possible scenario. Had Lucy finally lost interest in him, but was reluctant to tell him? *Well, I suppose it couldn't last anyway.* He would miss Lucy more than he thought possible. She is good company. He decided not to confront them on what he had overheard and to make the best of the here and now.

The next week, Anne sat alone – there was no sign of Lucy. When Tom enquired about Lucy, Anne merely said Lucy had a virus, but Tom suspected Anne wasn't telling the truth as she didn't quite look him in the eye when she spoke. The following week, Lucy was there and in good form, laughing and joking as usual, so much so that Tom dismissed his suspicions that Lucy was losing interest in him. Then again, Lucy missed a week, and still, Anne said it was a minor complaint that Lucy would recover from by next week. However, Tom thought something was going on – he felt sure of it, and it troubled him.

Then a few weeks later, Anne sat alone as Tom entered the cafe and she quickly called to him. The look on her face was the most serious he had ever seen Anne. Tom sat down opposite as the waitress brought his usual latte and a piece of cheesecake.

"I have some news about Lucy," Anne began. Tom looked up after taking a sip of coffee. Anne seemed to be struggling with what to say. "Oh, finish your latte first then I will tell you," she uttered, postponing what she needed to say concerning Lucy.

"What is it Anne? Is Lucy ill or had an accident?" Tom asked worriedly.

"No, nothing like that. It's nothing that serious. Well, maybe a little. Finish your coffee first then I'll tell you," Anne said still clearly struggling with what she had to tell Tom.

Tom finished his coffee and cheesecake in silence, concern for Lucy spoiling his usual enjoyment. Anne waited a few moments more before speaking.

"Lucy has breast cancer," she finally blurted out waiting Tom's reaction.

Tom's face had a look of pure anguish; his mouth dropped open. "Oh, I'm sorry," is all he could say.

"Lucy goes into hospital next week for the op to remove the lump. Luckily, they found it very early so she should be all right," Anne rushed on and was about to say more when Tom suddenly stood to leave.

"Give her my best wishes, and I hope she gets well soon," Tom said turning to leave.

Anne was dumbstruck at Tom's reaction. "Wait, don't you want to visit her in hospital?" she called after him, but he had gone without even looking back to inquire when and where to visit Lucy in hospital. Anne was furious; she thought she had got to know Tom well enough and also began to like him, but his reaction seemed off-hand and uncaring. He must have some idea of how much he meant to Lucy, even if it was just as a friend.

Anne sat beside Lucy's bed; there were flowers on the table and get-well cards from all her work colleagues. The operation had gone well, and the doctor had said there was no trace of the tumour remaining. Lucy sat up in bed drinking tea as she talked to Anne, asking her about how things were going at work.

Lucy was silent a moment then broached the question of what had been on her mind all the time she had been in the hospital. "Have you heard anything from Tom?"

Anne scowled, " I told you his reaction! He couldn't wait to get away when I told him; he never even asked what ward you were on, or for the visiting times. I didn't get a chance to tell him, he left that quick," replied Anne scornfully.

Lucy frowned, thinking to herself. *Well, he would know what ward to visit, and times.* Suddenly, she realised what that might mean. "Oh, of course! That's why he reacted as he did, the poor dear," she explained.

"What, are making excuses for him again? He doesn't deserve it, Lucy," Anne began before Lucy interrupted her.

"No, no, he told me his wife died from cancer five years ago, that's why," Lucy said.

"Oh," said Anne and shut her mouth.

"Yes, oh, indeed," said Lucy.

Tom entered the hospital with some trepidation; he brought some flowers and a card for Lucy. Several times, he thought about turning around and leaving again. The memories of his late wife came flooding back and seemed just as raw as ever he had to fight back the tears. *"Not again, not again,"* Tom kept repeating to himself then stopped in his tracks – a realisation dawned on him: *Why not again? It's not quite the same.* Lucy would get well again, not like his late wife. That thought made his heart jump with joy – it confirmed he loved Lucy. But did Lucy love him? He wasn't sure; he would soon find out. With renewed vigour in his step and hope in his heart, he entered the ward.

Anne turned hearing a familiar voice at the desk, talking to the ward nurse. Lucy, distracted, read one of the get-well-cards and paid no attention to who was speaking. "I think you have a visitor," Anne said with a sly smile.

Putting the card down, Lucy looked up to see Tom coming towards them and burst into tears of joy at the sight of him. If it not for Anne making her sit back, she would be out of bed and running to him.

"Oh, Tom, thank you for coming. I know it must have been hard for you," said Lucy wiping away tears.

"Shush now, Lucy," Tom replied, sitting at the bedside.

"I'll be off then. See you two tomorrow," Anne said, both Tom and Lucy nodded in agreement as Anne left.

Lucy noticed a difference in Tom and was pleasantly surprised when he took her hand in his.

"Get well soon, beautiful lady, so you can see my garden before the weather changes; it's supposed to be good weather for the next couple of weeks. Would you like to recuperate at my house?" Tom asked, hopefully.

Lucy beamed with delight sitting upright, she leaned forward and firmly kissed Tom on the cheek. Tom smiled. "I could get used to that," he said bashfully, his cheeks turning red a little.

It was a warm late autumn day as Lucy and Tom sat in the garden drinking coffee.

"I always wanted a garden of my own," said Lucy blissfully.

"Now you have one, my dear," replied Tom smiling.

Lucy felt in good health since the operation, and very happy, but hadn't quite got all that she wanted. Marriage was the first thing, and maybe it wasn't too late to have children. Lucy knew Tom had two daughters that lived away from home: one in France, the other in London. She would like to meet them, but all in good time. She knew Tom didn't want to rush things. She had learnt patience as far as Tom was concerned.

Three days before Christmas, the shopping mall was heaving with people rushing about, laden down with shopping and boxes containing Christmas gifts for loved ones. Lucy, Tom, Anne and her boyfriend sat at a table enjoying a coffee. One or two work colleagues from the department store came too. They all knew that Tom and Lucy were about to tell them something, and it could only mean one thing. Shirley, the manager of the coffee shop, came to join them as well.

Tom stood up, and they all fell silent waiting for him to speak. "Lucy and I are getting married in the spring," announced Tom grandly. They all clapped and congratulated the couple.

Lucy never felt so happy; she was to meet Tom's daughters before they wed. It would be a simple do with a church blessing, and a small reception afterwards – only close family and a few friends would be in attendance. Neither of them wanted a lot of fuss. Tom felt proud of his new love; it felt almost too good to believe, but true it was. He felt content and delighted in showing her to everyone he met.

Shirley offered to cater for their wedding, which they accepted. The reception would be held in the coffee shop. As Shirley watched the couple as they sat talking, she felt sure from the start that Lucy and Tom were meant to be together. To Shirley, the coffee shop meant more than just a place to have a coffee or tea and bite to eat. It was a place for people to come together and a chance to find happiness in the process.

The End

Elizabeth Sends Her Love

A thick fog descended, blanketing the surrounding countryside so densely that Pete couldn't see more than a few inches in front as he stepped from the car to retrieve his overnight bag and equipment from the boot. He stood for a moment, surveying the gloomy-looking manor house. No welcoming light seemed to show from within; Pete hefted his gear and strode to the door. He was about to drop his bag so he could knock, when the door opened and a slender woman stood outlined in the light from within.

"Miss Eleanor Chingley?" Pete said enquiringly.

"Yes, and you must be Peter Cherry, the ghost hunter," Eleanor answered.

"Yes, pleased to meet you, Miss Chingley. I was a little surprised to hear from you. I hadn't realised I had achieved such notoriety," Pete said.

"Oh, but you have. I have done my research into your background, that is why I asked for you," Eleanor replied, ushering Peter into the spacious sitting room.

Pete looked around as he set his equipment down; the room was a spacious sitting-cum-dining room, with a large dining table stood in the centre. On a side wall, a hearth with a log fire burned. At the opposite end from the entrance, a balconied stairway led to an overlooking landing, and several doors could be seen on the far wall. Other furnishings were sparsely placed around the room, and two exits besides the entrance led from the sitting room.

"Well, I'll show you to your room first, Peter, so that you can freshen up then we can have dinner. Oh and call me Eleanor," she said, smiling.

"Thank you ah... Eleanor," Pete answered. For the first time, he took a good look at his hostess as she led him to his room.

Pete guessed her age at somewhere between forty and fifty; she was a brunette with shoulder-length hair, blue eyes and she wore a creamy white full-length sleeveless gown that gently hugged her figure; there was a look of melancholy about her. He was surprised when he returned downstairs to see the dining table set and the meal ready and waiting. He hadn't seen or heard any servants or helpers.

"So where shall I set up my equipment Eleanor?" Pete asked as he set his knife and fork down on the empty plate. The meal had been excellent, and he already thanked her for it; he couldn't remember when he last had such a good meal.

"Oh in here will be fine, I'm sure, Peter," Eleanor replied with a smile that made her look all the more charming.

"What kind of manifestation is it you have been having? I mean, is it rattling chains, noises, apparitions that sort of thing?" Pete asked. He couldn't quite keep the scepticism from his voice; he hoped Eleanor hadn't noticed – she was a very gracious hostess and charming company.

In the five years Peter had been doing this job, he never once came across a real haunting – all of his cases had some sound explanation. Pete hoped that if he could at least find one valid case that there was life beyond death, then the loss of his wife would be less painful for him to bear. Pete no longer held any hope of finding proof of any kind.

He realised Eleanor hadn't answered, but seemed to be studying him with a sad, almost sympathetic, expression as if she understood what he was thinking.

"I think I will leave you to decide that for yourself, Peter. All I will tell you is it happens every year about this time," Eleanor finally answered. She rose from the table, and Pete followed suit.

"I will leave you to set up your equipment and bid you a goodnight, Pete," Eleanor concluded, turning towards the stairs.

"Goodnight, Eleanor, and thank you again for a lovely evening; I trust you will sleep well," Pete called. Eleanor strode up the stairs. Turning around, she smiled at him then, without another word, she entered the far room on the landing. Pete busily set his equipment up around the room which included cameras, motion detectors, temperature reading equipment, and light-sensitive and infrared equipment. When all was ready, Pete turned off the lights and made himself comfortable in an armchair and waited. Pete listened to the creak of timbers and the tell-tale sounds of small rodents scurrying about outside; an owl hooted in the night. All seemed normal, listening to these familiar sounds. He struggled to keep his eyes open, fitfully dozing, and starting awake at the slightest sound until eventually falling into a deep sleep. He woke with a start; grey light filtered through the curtains. He felt stiff and cold. Standing up, he rubbed his hands and knees to get the stiffness out; his watch said 7.15 a.m.

Then, Pete finally noticed his surroundings; his equipment was still there and working, but nothing else seemed the same. The room was dusty and cold and the dining table bare; the furnishings old and no sign of any recent fire in the hearth. Pete checked the other rooms – all were empty and didn't look used for years. Going upstairs, he checked his room – his bag was still where he had left it. Finally, he checked Eleanor's room that too was dusty and empty. Back in the sitting room, Peter examined his equipment; the cameras showed nothing but an empty house. Tom surmised nothing would show because, by the time he had set it up, it was already too late. It was then he noticed the piece of paper on the table where he had sat the night before. On it, in elegant handwriting, were the words: "Elizabeth sends her love."

Peter wiped a tear from his eye, overcome with emotions – both sadness and a kind of elation; at last, he had proof. As he drove onto the motorway, Pete considered returning to the old manor house next year; after all, Eleanor was such good company, and maybe he would have another message from his wife.

The End